THE BOOK OF BENJAMIN KARETH

"TO KNOW HIM, AND TO MAKE HIM KNOWN."

- PART 1 -
WHERE ALL JOURNEYS BEGIN

- BENJAMIN POTÉXANÁ KARETH -

THE BOOK OF BENJAMIN KARETH

"To Know Him, And To Make Him Known."

The ***Book Of Benjamin Kareth*** has one purpose and one purpose only:

"TO KNOW HIM AND MAKE HIM KNOWN."

The Him is ***Jesus Christ***.

This is the heart, the very core of every single one of the one hundred parts of ***The Book Of Benjamin Kareth***.

This is the meaning of the *"**Golden Thread**"* that runs from the back of the cover of part one all the way across each spine to the front cover of the hundredth part.

The "*White Thread*" that runs from the back of the first of the minor parts and runs to the front cover of the end of that minor part, signifies a section, season, or specific part of the whole.

No single part of **The Book Of Benjamin Kareth** is meant to stand on its own, all the parts fit together to form a whole. All the parts are like puzzle pieces, fitting together to form the ongoing testimony of a life touched by a relationship with and through the power of the Living God.

"When it was time for the sacrifice to be offered, Elijah the prophet came up and prayed, "O GOD, God of Abraham, Isaac, and Israel, make it known right now that you are God in Israel, that I am your servant, and that I'm doing what I'm doing under your orders. Answer me, GOD; O answer me and reveal to this people that you are GOD, the true God, and that you are giving these people another chance at repentance."" 1 Kings 18:36-37 MSG

THE MESSAGE

The Way, The Truth, And The Life

"FOR GOD SO LOVED THE WORLD THAT HE GAVE HIS ONE AND ONLY SON, THAT WHOEVER BELIEVES IN HIM SHALL NOT PERISH BUT HAVE ETERNAL LIFE. FOR GOD DID NOT SEND HIS SON INTO THE WORLD TO CONDEMN THE WORLD, BUT TO SAVE THE WORLD THROUGH HIM. WHOEVER BELIEVES IN HIM IS NOT CONDEMNED, BUT WHOEVER DOES NOT BELIEVE STANDS CONDEMNED ALREADY BECAUSE THEY HAVE NOT BELIEVED IN THE NAME OF GOD'S ONE AND ONLY SON. THIS IS THE VERDICT: LIGHT HAS COME INTO THE WORLD, BUT PEOPLE LOVED DARKNESS INSTEAD OF LIGHT BECAUSE THEIR DEEDS WERE EVIL. EVERYONE WHO DOES EVIL HATES THE LIGHT, AND WILL NOT COME INTO THE LIGHT FOR FEAR THAT THEIR DEEDS WILL BE EXPOSED. BUT WHOEVER LIVES BY THE TRUTH COMES INTO THE LIGHT, SO THAT IT MAY BE SEEN PLAINLY THAT WHAT THEY HAVE DONE HAS BEEN DONE IN THE SIGHT OF GOD." JOHN 3:16-21 NIVW

"IF YOU DECLARE WITH YOUR MOUTH, "JESUS IS LORD," AND BELIEVE IN YOUR HEART THAT GOD RAISED HIM FROM THE DEAD, YOU WILL BE SAVED. FOR IT IS WITH YOUR HEART THAT YOU BELIEVE AND ARE JUSTIFIED, AND IT IS WITH YOUR MOUTH THAT YOU PROFESS YOUR FAITH AND ARE SAVED. AS SCRIPTURE SAYS, "ANYONE WHO BELIEVES IN HIM WILL NEVER BE PUT TO SHAME." FOR THERE IS NO DIFFERENCE BETWEEN JEW AND GENTILE—THE SAME LORD IS LORD OF ALL AND RICHLY BLESSES ALL WHO CALL ON HIM, FOR, "EVERYONE WHO CALLS ON THE NAME OF THE LORD WILL BE SAVED."" ROMANS 10:9-13 NIV

Jesus Christ is the answer to every question you've ever had. When you hear that name, you feel a beat, a flutter in your heart. Something stirs. When you were born, you had a hole in you. A hole that only Jesus could fill. You've spent your life searching for something to fill it with... and nothing has filled it.

Jesus is the way, the truth, and the life. No one comes to the Father but by Him. Jesus was born completely man and completely God. He lived a human life, suffered as we do, tempted as we are, and he hungered and thirst just like us. Jesus gave up the glory of heaven to come down to dwell with us.

And He chose to die for us... perfect and without sin... to pay the price for our sins. He was nailed to a cross, His body broken, He died. In that moment, the price of your sin was paid. The barrier between God and us was torn in two. And after three days, Jesus through the Power of the Holy Spirit, rose again. He was resurrected... destroying the power of death forever. And He went back into Heaven to be with the Father. After He returned to Heaven He sent His Holy Spirit down to fill us and guide us as He had promised He would.

The gospel is simple. God created us to have choice and to have choice we had to be created into a world with true choice. The choice between our own way and His. He laid out the law that governs and judges our sin. Sin is any action or thought that is not done by faith in Him. Faith is trust and believe that He alone is God and that He loves us and knows best. So, through the law, God declared war with our sin nature, our hellbent core that is determined to choose self. And death was the judgement for sin.

And God declared that the only way back to Him was through a sacrifice. Through death, the very punishment for sin, something or someone that was pure had to be offered up and their blood shed to make us right before God. But God had a plan. He Himself came to earth, Jesus arrived, lived, suffered and died for us. So God laid the blood price for our sins and through Jesus made a way back into relationship with Him. And that way is a free gift to anyone who will simply believe. Believe is just a personal choice to place trust in something outside ourselves. And bam... Back in relationships with God. Then God does the rest of the work to draw you back to Him, His way, each day.

So those who have not put their faith and trust in God through Jesus are bound and judged by the law. And it is a law of rationality, reason, and death. Self-justification bring no rest. Self-righteousness brings only toil and pain. Selfishness is a cancer that in the end destroys everything in your life.

Faith and believe in Jesus doesn't bring instant perfection. It begins the work of God in your life, the work of sanctification. Sanctification is a process, it requires yielding to the every active hand on God in your life. It takes trust, day after day after day, through obedience. It takes a heart that says, "God you are God and I am not. You know the better way, so lead me in it." And He does.

I am not perfect, no far from it. My heart daily fails and betrays me and my faith. My heart, the parts that have yet to be yielded and surrendered, wage a war against the parts that have been laid down and transformed.

So if you have placed your faith in Jesus, accepted Him as your savior, sit back, and watch God be God. Your life will never be the same. God will began a good work in you and that work won't end till you die here and arrive there.

If you don't know Jesus as your personal savior, I'd like to lead you in a prayer. It's a simple prayer, but it is the most powerful prayer you'll ever pray. Praying is just talking to God.

So pray this out loud:

"Jesus, I believe you came to earth and lived. I believe you died for my sins. I accept your forgiveness for my sins and accept the gift of eternal life! Come into my heart and make it your home. Fill me with your Holy Spirit! Take away my sins and trade them for life in you! Amen."

Welcome to the greatest family on earth! We are so excited to have you be our brother or sister! God has big plans for you! Believe it!

DEDICATION

DEDICATED TO THE NAME OF THE LIVING GOD

I would like to dedicate this book to the Name of the Lord. The great I AM. The one and only true living God. To Jesus Christ the King of Kings, and the Lord of Lords, whose name is above all others. To the Holy Spirit. There has never been or will ever be anyone like Him. Enthroned forever. Without His unfailing love this book would never have been written and it is written for the sole purpose of bringing glory to His great Name.

I AM, THAT I AM

Before you can have a relationship with someone you must first know their name...

In the Bible Moses asks God what's His name:

MOSES SAID TO GOD, "SUPPOSE I GO TO THE ISRAELITES AND SAY TO THEM, `THE GOD OF YOUR FATHERS HAS SENT ME TO YOU,' AND THEY ASK ME, `WHAT IS HIS NAME?' THEN WHAT SHALL I TELL THEM?" EXODUS 3:13

God's Response:

GOD SAID TO MOSES, "I AM WHO I AM. THIS IS WHAT YOU ARE TO SAY TO THE ISRAELITES: `I AM HAS SENT ME TO YOU.'" EXODUS 3:14

This book bears the Name of the Living God, the one, true God. He is the creator of all things both in heaven and on earth. He was, He is, and He is always. The following can be collectively described as the Name of the Living God, collected from the pages of the Bible:

He is the great I AM. He is Elohim: God, Judge, Creator. He is Yahweh: Lord, Jehovah. He is El Elyon: Most High God. He is Adonai: LORD, Master. He is El Shaddai: LORD God Almighty. He is El Olam: The Everlasting God, the God of Eternity, the God of the Universe, the God of Ancient Days. He is Jehovah Jireh: the LORD will provide. He is The Shiloh: The Peacemaker. He is Jehovah Rapha: The LORD that heals. He is Jehovah Nissi: The LORD My Banner, The LORD My Miracle. He is Qanna: Jealous. He is Jehovah M'Kaddesh: The LORD Who Sanctifies You, The LORD Who Makes Holy. He is A Star, A Scepter Out Of Israel, The Accursed Of God, The Captain Of The Host Of The LORD. He is Jehovah Shalom: The LORD is Peace.

He is Jehovah Sabaoth: The LORD of Hosts, The LORD of Powers. He is the Rock of My Salvation. He is The Light of The Morning When The Sun Rises, A Morning Without Clouds. He is The Daysmen, The Interpreter, My Rock, My Redeemer. He is Crowned With A Crown Of Pure Gold, The Most Blessed Forever. He is The Forsaken, A Worm, And No Man. He is Jehovah Raah: The LORD My Shepherd. He is My Restorer, The King of Glory, He Who Sitteth King Forever. He is A Stranger, An Alien. He is My Strong Rock, My Rock And My Fortress, Fairer Than The Children Of Men, The Rock That Is Higher Than I, The Rock Of My Strength, The Rock Of Habitation. He is As Rain Upon The Mown Grass, As Showers That Water The Earth, The Rock of My Heart.

He is The Shield, The Rock of My Refuge, The King And Priest After The Order Of Melchizedek. He is A Brother Born For Adversity, The Friend That Loveth At All Times, A Stone Of Grace, A Friend That Sticketh Closer Than A Brother. He is As Ointment Poured Forth, My Well Beloved, A Bundle Of Myrrh, A Cluster Of Henna Blooms, The Rose of Sharron. He is The Lily of

The Valley, The Chiefest Among Ten Thousand. His Countenance Is As Lebanon. Yea, He Is Altogether Lovely. He is My Beloved and My Friend. He is Holy, Holy, Holy. He is A Sanctuary. He is A Great Light, A Son Given, The Mighty God. He is The Father Of Eternity, A Child Born.

He is The Prince Of Peace. He is An Ensign Of The People, The Nail Fastened In A Sure Place. He is A Strength To The Poor, The Strength To The Needy In Distress. He is A Shadow From The Heat, The Refuge From The Storm. He is The Rock Of Ages, A Crown of Glory And Beauty. He is A Stone, A Tried Stone, A Covert From The Tempest. He is As Rivers Of Water In A Dry Place, As The Shadow Of A Great Rock In A Weary Land, As A Hiding Place From The Wind. He is The King In His Beauty, My Leader, The Everlasting God. He is Mine Elect In Whom My Soul Delighteth. He is A Light Of The Gentiles, A Covenant Of The People, The Polished Shaft.

He is Glorious, The Holy One Of Israel.

He is A Man Of Sorrows, Despised, Rejected, Stricken, Smitten, Wounded, Bruised, Oppressed. He is My Portion, My Maker, My Husband. He is The God Of The Whole Earth, The Witness To His People. He is A Leader, A Commander. He is The Redeemer. He is Mighty, My Physician. He is Jehovah Tsidkenu: The LORD Our Righteousness. He is David Their King, My Resting Place, My Feeder, The Plant Of Renown. He is Jehovah Shammah: The LORD Is There. He is The Prince of Princes, The Messiah, The Prince. He is The Strength Of The Children Of Israel, The Hope of Thy People, The Ruler. He is The King Over All The Earth. He is A Refiner's Fire, Fuller's Soap, My Refiner, My Purifier. He is The Son of Righteousness. He is Jesus, Yeshua... Salvation. He is Emmanuel: God With Us.

He is Born As The King Of The Jews, The Governor, The Nazarene, The Bridegroom. He is Meek, Lowly. He is The One Of Whom The Father Says, "My Beloved, In Whom My Soul Is Well Pleased." He is The Son Of The

Living God, Jesus, The Christ. He is The Rock, The Builder, The Prophet Of Nazareth. He is Betrayed, Mocked, Crucified, The Holy One Of God. He is My Brother, The Carpenter, His Life Is A Ransom. He is The Son Of The Blessed, The Son Of The Highest, God My Savior. He is The Horn Of Salvation, The Dayspring From On High, A Savior, Which Is Christ The Lord. He is The Salvation Of God. He is The Glory Of Thy People Israel, Lord of The Sabbath, My Healer. He is The Christ of God, My Servant. He is The Chosen Of God. He is Risen. He is A Prophet Mighty In Deed And Word.

He is The Word, The Word That Was With God, The Word That Was God. He is The Light Of Men, The True Light, The Word That Was Made Flesh. He is The Only Begotten Son Which Is In The Bosom Of The Father. He is The Lamb of God, My Teacher, The Gift Of God. He is Messiah, The Bread Of God, The Bread Of Life. He is My Meat, My Drink, The Light Of The World. He is The Door Of The Sheep, The Good Shepherd That Laid Down

His Life, The Sent Of The Father. He is The Resurrection, The King Of The Daughter Of Zion. He is The Corn Of Wheat, The Light, My LORD, Master. He is My Example. He is The Way, The Truth, The Life. He is The Vine, Scourged, Crowned With A Crown Of Thorns. He is Crucified As The King Of The Jews, Exalted, Glorified. He is The Holy One And The Just, The Prince Of Life, The Anointed.

He is The Prince And A Savior, LORD Jesus, LORD of All. He is The Judge, Jesus Of Nazareth, The Mercy Seat. He is Jesus Christ Our LORD, The Firstborn Among Many Brethren, Over All, God Blessed Forever. He is LORD Over All, The Deliverer, LORD Both Of The Dead And Living. He is The Minister Of The Circumcision, My Wisdom, My Righteousness. He is My Sanctification, My Redemption. He is The Foundation, My Passover, That Spiritual Rock. He is The Head Of Every Man, The Firstfruits Of Them That Slept. He is The Last Adam, The Quickening Spirit, The Image Of God. He is His Unspeakable Gift, My Peace,

The Offering, The Sacrifice.

He is The Head Over All Things To The Church, He That Filleth All In All, A Servant, Who Humbled Himself Unto Death, Even Death On A Cross. He is The LORD Jesus Christ, The Image Of The Invisible God, The First Born Of Every Creature. He is The Creator Of All Things. He is The First Born From The Dead, The Head of the Body, The Church. He is The Head of All Principalities And Powers. He is My All In All. He is Our Lord Jesus Christ Himself, LORD Of Peace, LORD Of Hope. He is God Manifest In The Flesh, The Justified, The Mediator. He is The Righteous Judge, The Great God And Our Savior Jesus Christ. He is Obedient, And His Throne Is For Ever And Ever. He is The Upholder Of All Things, The Express Image Of His Person. He is The Brightness of His Glory, Jesus Christ, The Same Yesterday, Today, And Forever. He is The Shepherd Of The Sheep, The Great Shepherd That Was Brought Again From The Dead, The Minister Of The Sanctuary, And Of The True

Tabernacle, And His Flesh Is The Veil Which Was Rent In Two. He is The Altar, The Offerer, The Forerunner For Us. He is Entered, Even Jesus, The Priest, The High Priest, The Great High Priest.

He is The Intercessor, The Surety, The Covenanter. He is The Captain Of Salvation, The Author And Finisher Of Faith. He is The King Of Righteousness, The King Of Peace. He is Crowned with Glory And Honor, The Tempted. He is The Merciful, The Faithful. He is Holy, Harmless. He is Undefiled, The Separate, The Perfect. He is My Helper, The Lamb Without Blemish And Without Spot, The Living Stone. He is A Chief Cornerstone, A Precious Stone, Guileless. He is Reviled, The Chief Shepherd, That Shall Again Appear. He is The Day Star, My Savior, The Word Of Life. He is The Life, That Eternal Life Which Was With The Father.

He is Jesus Christ The Righteous, The Savior Of The World. He is The True God. He is The Advocate. He is Jesus

Christ, The First Begotten Of The Dead, The Prince Of The Kings Of The Earth. He is The Almighty Which Is, And Which Was, And Which Is To Come. He is The Beginning And The End, The Alpha And The Omega, The First and The Last. He is He That Liveth, The Tree Of Life, The Hidden Manna. He is The Faithful And True Witness, The Amen. He is The Beginning Of The Creation Of God, The Lion Of The Tribe Of Judah. He is The Lamb That Was Slain, The Lamb In The Midst Of The Throne.

He is The Lamb Slain. He is The King of Saints, King Of Nations. He is LORD of Lords. He is Faithful and True. He is Crowned With Many Crowns, The Word Of God. He is The King of Kings, The Temple. He is The Bright And Morning Star.

MY PRAYER AS YOU READ

This is the prayer covering for this book, a prayer prayed by me, Benjamin Potexana Kareth, to God, the living God, the Father, through Jesus, the One and Only Son, and by the power of the Holy Spirit.

"Father, I thank you that you always hear me. I thank you for leading this person here, the person reading this. Thank you for what you are about to do in their lives through the words in this book. Take this book as my offering to you, may it bring your Great Name glory, honor, and praise. May I be hidden among these pages and may you be seen! May my name be forgotten and yours be remembered forever! Draw this reader to you and show them who you are! I thank you for the gift of your Word. It is a lamp to my feet and a light to my path. I thank you for the authority that you have given me through the victory of my King Jesus Christ, your son. I speak life

over anyone who reads this book. From the first page of it to the last I speak protection over anyone who reads this book. You said that whatever I bind on earth will be bound in heaven. So in the name of Jesus Christ, your Son, my King, I bind every lie of the enemy that would try to sneak in and steal what you would say though the words of this book. You also said that whatever I loose on earth will be loosed in heaven. So in the name of Jesus Christ, your Son, my King, I loose life into anyone who reads this book. I break off any chains of the enemy that have bound their soul. I speak freedom over them. Give them ears to hear and eyes to see what you would say to them through this book. From page one to the last page, let you Great Name be glorified. I thank you the enemy has been defeated. I ask all this in the most powerful name of your son Jesus Christ. Amen."

- Benjamin Potexana Kareth

THE BOOK OF BENJAMIN KARETH

"TO KNOW HIM, AND TO MAKE HIM KNOWN."

- PART 001 -
WHERE ALL JOURNEYS BEGIN

- BENJAMIN POTÉXANÁ KARETH -

Table Of Contents

FIELD

It had been a rough day, and everything seemed to have gone wrong at work. No one was happy and everything I tried to do just seemed to fall apart. I left work and drove the thirty-minute commute home, passing from the city where I worked out into the country where my small house sat.

I enjoyed living far from the busyness of the city and I loved living alone. I had never been very social, and it seemed that the few friends I had at work, if I could call them that, kept a respectable distance. Being alone was safe. I couldn't hurt anyone, and I couldn't be hurt. I was determined to live the rest of my life away from all the stress and drama of others. After setting my briefcase down and changing into some simple jeans and a t-shirt, I quickly ate some leftovers and left the house. I walked out into the wide field that surrounded my house. This was my daily ritual. It calmed me down.

The sun was beginning to set, casting long shadows across the grass. I was barefoot. There was nothing better than the feel of the grass beneath my feet. Nature was so peaceful. It was early spring and the trees surrounding the field were bright green. Flowers bloomed everywhere. Birds sang loudly and flew overhead. Squirrels ran here and there in the trees. I took it all in... let it calm me. I needed time. Time to reflect. Time to recharge. Time to put things into perspective, some called it meditation, but for me it was my time to listen. When I spent time with God, all I did was listen. He had been very quiet lately, but with God it seemed that just spending time with Him was what he wanted most from me. I don't think I ever prayed. He knew what I was going to ask, so why ask? 'Be still and know that I am God,' I thought to myself and that's what I planned to do this evening. I stepped into the tall, green grass that was in the center of the field. This was my secret place, the place where I was completely secluded, away from everyone and everything. This was my mountaintop. I dropped to my knees, placed both hands on the ground in front of me, and closed my eyes. I let my day fade from my mind. I let my problems shrink and become insignificant. I cleared my mind of all the 'me' I could... and then I waited.

The breeze across the field brushed my skin. I heard the birds calling from somewhere in the distance. Then... there was just stillness. Darkness enclosed my mind, pulled me down and down. It surrounded me, swirled through me. I felt my sprit rising, growing in me... taking control. My spirit rose and I let go of all the flesh that held me back.

In my spirit's eyes I stood to my feet. The field was ablaze with the rose-red colors of the spiritual world. The blue breeze rushed across it. The brilliant white of the sky stretched out above me and the darkness of the cold earth was beneath my feet. I stretched my spirit. Secret place. I waited for God... I reached for Him, for the sweetness of His love. I felt it and, like a rush of a floodgate being released, He was there with me. My spirit warmed all over as His love replaced all that I was. It consumed me. I felt all the 'me' being replaced with Him. To know God was to know love and peace. I stood for a long time there with Him... just basking in the love and acceptance.

Finally, I reached for God with all I was... and felt Him respond in kind. I heard His still small voice echo through me, "I have something to show you." There was a pause and then He asked me, "Do you trust me?"

"Always." I replied with my mind in that place. "Do you trust me?" He asked again. This time I didn't just hear His question... I felt it. The words passed through my mind and sent chills down my spine. This wasn't simply a question. There was meaning there, behind those words. Did I trust him? Not just in my life, but with my life... with all I was. This wasn't a normal meeting with Him... this was serious... significant. I never claimed to know God perfectly, but I had spent enough time with Him to know that when He asked me this question now it would mean that I would face something very, very difficult. Different. My mind spun. 'Something to show you?' His words echoed in my mind. They seared through me, burned me from the inside out. I felt pain, and I knew that this was only a small taste of what I would face if I chose to say yes again. He was asking me to let go... of everything. I belonged to God. I was His. To be used as He willed. I knew I was rebellious. I fought Him often and challenged His will in my life. I longed to be home with Him, finally at peace forever, but somehow that longing felt selfish to me. There was so much I knew that He wanted from my life, and I had told Him that I would do anything He asked. I knew my life was far from perfect, I had strayed from Him so many times in the thirty years of life He had given me, but He was always patient and continued to love and guide me on this journey with Him.

He had shown me a lot in the past few years, things I rarely shared with others. But this... this was different. This, whatever He wanted to show me now, would be hard... harder than anything I had ever experienced before. I made my choice, as I knew I always would.

I formed the reply in my mind to Him, "Yes. I trust you with all my heart. I trust you with my life, my future, and all that is within me."

I felt His love surround me. It squeezed me tight in what I knew to be a hug. His still small voice whispered, "Endure. I have made you strong and prepared you for such a time as this. Never forget that I am always with you." And then He was gone.

I stood there alone and unable to feel Him anymore. From behind my eyelids the light around me faded suddenly. I snapped back to myself and threw my eyes open. Looking up, I saw black clouds hurrying across the sky toward me. They passed above me and surrounded the field where I knelt. There was a flash... lightning. A loud boom of thunder shook the ground beneath me. I stood to my feet and turned to run back to the house should rain begin to fall. I froze. I watched the darkness swirl above me. It shimmered and shone as it spun, like a dark pearl spinning in the sky.

There was another blinding flash, and I was thrown backwards off my feet and landed hard on my back.

I lay there stunned.

Slowly I pulled myself up on my hands...

then I saw them.

Surrounding me on every side were dark creatures. Their faces twisted into insane smiles. Their wings were broken and twisted up from their backs. Their arms were stunted and misshapen and blood dripped from their clawed hands. They wore pitch black, tattered robes and were laughing at me... pointing at me... screaming curses at me. Their hatred of me was like heat, pure heat against my soul, against my skin.

Terror flooded me. What should I do? I could feel the evil pouring from them. I could taste it in the air.

I started to cry out to God, but my mouth wouldn't form the words. Was this a dream? Wake up Kail... wake up. I reached up, closed my eyes, and rubbed my face. I opened them again... not a dream. A nightmare.

I jumped to my feet and spun in circles. They were everywhere, laughing and pointing at me. Then I saw him... the one that stood taller than the others. He stepped out from the circle toward me, and, as he walked toward me, he transformed. One second, he resembled the others and the next he was shining. His wings straightened and stretched out behind and around him. His eyes glimmered and his smile widened. His dark hair shined and gleamed, going from pitch black to brilliant white. He was almost... beautiful. The features of his face softened. He carried a harp that gleamed black and was attached to his belt. The claws on his hands withdrew and his nails became gleaming silver. His tattered robes became shimmering gold armor plating. He was an angel. Not just any angel, but a powerful one... so beautiful... I wanted to do anything for him. His eyes, those gleaming, shining white eyes, were fixed on me as he came. Then he spoke, no... he sang to me... "You were the one." At first it was a whisper, but it grew in volume each time he sang it. "You were the one!" He sang those words to all those that surrounded us, pointing at me. It was a mocking, accusing song. He glided as he walked, and there was so much beauty as he moved. I was mesmerized as he sang and glided forward. Back and forth he shifted... I couldn't take my eyes off him. "You were the one." He sang, in a voice that was so perfect, so beautiful, that it seemed to caress my ears. I wanted to hear more. I wanted to listen to him forever. As he walked forward, darkness trailed behind him like a low fog across the grass. As the fog passed over the ground, the grass died and withered beneath him.

"You were the one." He sang again. His song was entrancing. It wrapped and swirled around me. I was stunned. I tried to step back and away but my legs wouldn't move. I swayed back and forth with the rhythm of his song.

"He was the one." He sang to the others. They echoed him, not in song but with low growls. "He was the one." The laughed and hooted. They pointed at me and shared dark whispers to each other. They mocked and growled.

"He doesn't even know it! Does he?" the dark creatures howled.

"You were the one who did it... But you know that... don't you?" He sang, and with every word he accused me.

"It was you. You did it. You think you didn't do it? Think you weren't there? So... innocent, ha!" He sang on and raised his beautifully dark hand.

He pointed at me. "You were there!" He screamed and threw back his head in laughter. Then he stopped suddenly and looked down at me. His smile twisted into a half grin and his eyes glinted.

"You think it was me, don't you?" He asked. "You think it was me?"

More laughter.

"He thinks it was me!" he called to the others.

Another wave of laughter and mocking surged through the others. Tears welled up in my eyes and the truth of his words flooded me. Flashes of a garden, a piece of fruit, gold coins, a whip, clothes torn and cast on the ground, and of a cross on a hill pounded my mind. I panicked. Terror surrounded me and evil flooded me.

Tears poured and burned my eyes. I fell to my knees and wept.

I looked up and screamed, "I wasn't there! I didn't do it! How could I? I wasn't even born yet?" I railed against his accusations. I begged him, "Let me go! I didn't do it. I wasn't the one."

The instant those words left my mouth a crack of thunder rocked the field. I felt God turn away. All light left in an instant. I looked up at the sky, looked up at the wall of darkness. Then... I knew. Knowledge flooded me. I was the one. I had been there. I looked back down at the dark one, my accuser.

He now stood a few feet from me with his arm stretched out toward me. "Come." He sang. "Come with me and I'll show you what you've done. Just reach out and give me your hand. I'll do better than show you... I promise."

I slowly reached up and placed my hand in his. He gripped it hard and twisted my arm, bringing me down to my knees. He threw back his head and howled to the darkness. "So be it." He snarled. He leaned down close to my face, looked me deep in the eyes, and whispered, "I'll do better than show you... I'll make you... re-live it."

GARDEN

The dark one shoved me away from him and I fell backward with such force that I was thrown from my knees backward. I fell. All was dark. I felt nothing. Everything was black. I fell for what seemed like hours or maybe days. I had no concept of time or location. Then I hit. The force of the sudden stop stunned me. All my senses overloaded. My eyes were shut tight. My ears hummed. Then slowly everything returned to normal... and I began to feel and hear again.

With my eyes still held shut, I could feel that I was lying on my back. I felt no clothing but was warm. I lay on... grass. It was smooth and soft against my bare skin. I took a breath and the air that filled my lungs was rich and clean. A million different smells flooded my senses: flowers, water, and trees... all of them smelled richly in the air. It felt like I was waking from a nightmare and into the most wonderful dream.

Then I felt it. Somewhere close, someone very familiar was hovering. A presence. I knew that feeling… the light and the warmth… the love. The source of everything… God.

I threw my eyes open. I was looking upward at the sky. Gentle, white clouds lazily crossed the brilliant, blue sky above me. I sat up, feeling my body respond in an instant. My muscles responded without any aches or pains. I looked around. I was in a field, no… a garden. There were trees and bushes everywhere… and animals. All kinds of animals wondered around. I wasn't in my field anymore. My memories of the life I'd lived faded. I closed my eyes, shook my head, and slowly opened them to this new life.

I was this man… in this place.

Then I saw Him. God. Indescribable. Brilliant light surrounded Him. I should have fallen to my face from the glory that spilled from around Him, but, without hesitation, I leapt to my feet and ran. I ran over to where He hovered, I waved to Him like He was my dearest friend. I stopped close to Him and bowed deep. I knew Him. We were friends and He loved me. He had created me. He had made me to be his companion.

His smile was deep as I stood before Him, and the look of a proud father was on His face. He was so proud of me. All of this I knew... simply because... it just was.

Then He spoke, "Adam." There was so much love in the way He said my name. I had just been created. "Welcome to the garden I have created for you," He said with such kindness in His voice.

I smiled deep and breathed in the air around me. I looked around at the green landscape of trees and rolling hills. Color everywhere. Time didn't matter here, and, for what seemed like an endless number of days, we talked and walked through the garden. He showed me all of it... the animals... the trees... the bushes. He taught me everything I would need to know to take care of it. This was my home. I named all the animals, tasted each fruit, and tended to everything. God would come each day in the cool of the afternoon to walk and talk with me.

We laughed together.

Each day seemed longer and longer. Each animal had a mate. They all seemed so happy with one another, but I was… alone. There was no 'other' for me. I was very happy but something… something was missing. I enjoyed the time with God and although I knew I was his, I felt a hole in myself. Tending the garden was a lot of work and it was almost too much for me to do by myself. I didn't have anyone to help me.

One day when God and I were walking though the garden He said, "We have not found you a suitable helper, so I am going to create one for you." I turned to him and suddenly felt very sleepy. I lay down on the ground and curled up. I was covered in warmth. I closed my eyes and fell into a very deep sleep.

I awoke sometime later. I stretched and stood to my feet. Something was missing. I looked down at my side. I ran my fingers across the small red line that traced my side… a rib was missing. I felt God there. I turned and saw Him. My mouth dropped open.

Standing with him was the most beautiful creature I had ever seen. She was human like me. Her hair was long and fell in front of her beautiful body. She was clothed in brilliant light like me. Her eyes were a brilliant green.

God spoke, "You now have a helper, taken from your own body. You both shall tend the garden together and eat whatever you want of the fruit here. There is only one tree that you shall never eat of, the Tree of the Knowledge of Good and Evil, for the day you eat from that tree you will surely die."

I knew that tree well. It sat in the center of the garden next to the Tree of Life. I trusted Him and had never considered eating that fruit. This was not the first time He had warned me not to eat of the Tree of the Knowledge of Good and Evil. When He had first created me, He had given me the same warning.

I ate from the Tree of Life daily. Its fruit was sweeter than all the rest and satisfied my hunger with just one bite. As the fruit passed my lips, I always felt a surge of life much like the first breathe I had ever taken when I was created. I had never been tempted to eat from the other fruit. I trusted God... and if He had a reason for me NOT to do something... I obeyed.

Each day passed in peace in that garden.

Eve and I were happy. We walked and talked with God every day. We even laughed so much that I looked forward to the time we had with Him. Everything was great, and I couldn't ask for anything more from the life that had been given to me.

FALL

I woke one day to the brilliant light of the sun shining on my skin. Its warmth filled me and gave me pleasure. I rolled away from where Eve still slept and got to my feet. I stretched big and thought of what I needed to do today. Today was the day that Eve and I would take care of the west side of the garden. It was a long walk and I wanted to get a head start on my work. I looked down at Eve as she continued to sleep deeply. She was so beautiful, shining in her brilliance and making her sweet sounds of sleep. After watching her for a while, I decided to let her sleep a bit longer. I knew she would come find me when she awoke.
I set off toward the western part of the garden. The morning walk was pleasant. The animals came, as they always did, and greeted me. They walked with me, and we talked of all the new things going on. Great, the male lion, talked for a long time about how his coat was shedding

and how it was scattered all around
his den. I laughed at the thought of this
because I knew how Shebra, his mate,
spent most of her day cleaning their den.
I arrived and began my days' work.
As the sun passed overhead and the day
lengthened,
I wondered where Eve was. She had not
joined me in my work this morning and
I was beginning to feel something I had
never felt before… something was not
right. After a while longer, I began to
look for her. She was not where we had
slept the night before. I looked for a long
time before I found her.
As I walked up the hill in the center of
the garden, I saw her standing next to
the Tree of the Knowledge of Good and
Evil. She was talking with one of the
serpents that lived in the garden. Sly
was his name. As I approached them, I
overheard their conversation…
"But did He really say that you shouldn't
eat of any tree in the garden?" The
serpent hissed to Eve. "Didn't he create
it all for you? Didn't He want you to
taste all the beautifully, sweet fruit He
has made? Everything He has created

is so wonderful, would He really create something that would harm or kill you?" Eve replied, "He did tell us to eat of any tree in the garden, but the only tree He commanded us not to eat of was this tree. He said that we should not even touch it, or we would surely die."

The serpent let out a mocking hiss and threw his head back and laughed. Then he looked Eve deep in the eyes and drew very close to her face, he looked around, then said in a low, seductive hiss, "You will not surely die. For God knows that when you eat of this fruit your eyes will be opened. You will know everything that He knows, and you will be like Him. You will know what good and evil are. Won't you rise to where God is and become like him? Aren't you created in His image? Didn't He create you to be like Him?"

As I approached where they stood, I watched Eve look at the fruit. "It does look very good. I bet it tastes great and I do want to gain its wisdom and be like God." She looked at me and then reached out and took a piece of the fruit in her hand. I watched her, fascinated at what she was about to do. She bit down on it, chewed for a moment then swallowed. Her eyes widened, "It is so wonderful." She exclaimed. She turned quickly and handed the fruit to me. "Try it! Oh, you must try some Adam." I took the fruit from her and took a bite. I felt its sweetness in my mouth. I swallowed down the bite. It glided and sank into me. Then something changed. Something was wrong. My eyes were suddenly opened. My mind twirled with the changes… with the knowledge. Everything was clear to me in an instant. What we had done was very wrong. I looked at Eve and watched as the light faded from her beautiful form. She was naked. Exposed. I looked her form over and something I had never felt came over me. I wanted her. She was mine and I wanted to have her. Her curves ignited a passion in me. My body hungered for her. She was created to please me. She looked back at me and stared. I looked down to see what she was looking at. The light had faded from me as well. I was naked and exposed. I knew this was all so very wrong. What had we

done? What had she made me do?
Anger rose in me. Rage flooded my head
and blinded me. I looked at Eve and
suddenly hated her. She had made me do
this! She was the one…
I threw the fruit against the trunk of the
tree, and it broke into a million pieces.
I snarled at her, and she cowered away
from me in fear.
"Look what you've done!" I yelled at her.
I wanted to kill her. I wanted to make
all of this go away and be right again.
"What have you done to us? You were
supposed to love me!" I raged against
her. I grabbed her by the arm and threw
her to the ground. "I wish you were
dead, woman! Make this all right!" Tears
of anger stung my eyes. I suddenly felt
horribly ashamed of having lashed out
at her. All these feelings were so new to
me. I didn't understand anything I felt.
My head spun. I crouched on the ground
and closed my eyes. Eve shrieked and
began to cry. I know she cried out for
me to stop; she blamed the serpent with
every word she spoke.
My head spun… What had I done?
A jolt of energy struck me. I was thrown

backward out of Adam and onto the ground. My life flooded back to me. My job in the city, my little house in the country, the field where I had been, and the evil, mocking creatures flooded my mind as my memories from my life came back to me.

I felt different... heavy... constricted. I looked down and saw that black chains were now surrounding my waist, my wrists, my neck, and my feet. All the chains were connected to another large one. I followed where it led and saw him.

Holding the end of the large chain was the dark one from the field. He was standing next to me. Darkness flooded out of him and surrounded the scene that stood before me. There were other dark creatures there with him. They circled Adam and Eve, and all railed in their own dark glory at what had just taken place.

The dark one pulled my chain and I fell to my knees. He sang again, "You were there! You were the one! You did it! Now you see... don't you?" On and on he mocked and accused me. The others laughed and joined him. They cried out to their master, 'They are ours now, we own them forever!'

I watched in horror as I stood witnessing the final moments of the fall of mankind. I looked up to where Adam and Eve stood. The glorious light that had clothed them before was gone. It had faded. They were now wrapped in the black chains that also encompassed and enslaved me. I knelt there beside the dark one with tears pouring from my eyes. The pain of what I had done was infinite. It ripped through me in waves. I had done what God had commanded me not to do. I had eaten the fruit. My small life... every choice I'd made against the will of God... it all was connected... all the same sin... I wept and wept. The dark one continued his jubilation at my fall. All I could do now is watch as the scene continued before me.

Lust, a dark and twisted creature, came forward from the circle and thrust his twisted blade into Adam's mind. He whispered into his ear thoughts. I watched as Adam stared at Eve's naked form and watched as his mind twisted with dark and lustful thoughts. Beautiful desire turned to envious lust. I watched as Lust laughed aloud and mocked at the heavens. He let out a cry of victory and screamed, "He's mine now!" He pulled his blade from Adam's mind and returned to the circle to continue his mocking.

I watched in horror as each of the prime sins took turns twisting Adam's mind. They stuck him and whispered to him. They laughed and cried out their victories, "What God created for himself, we took so easily! Such weak creations!" I watched as Adam stopped his attack on Eve and stood to his feet. He looked up at the sun. "Quickly!" He yelled at Eve and pulled her to her feet. "God is coming to walk with us. We must hide! We must find a way to cover ourselves." Eve nodded her head. They ran through the garden, looking for some way to hide their shame and nakedness. They found fig leaves that would cover them. Quickly they crafted clothes out of the leaves and placed it over their bodies. I was drug along behind the dark one by the chains that bound me now. I was

unable to break them. I was helpless
now. I was forced to watch through my
tear-stained eyes.

After they had finished covering
themselves, Adam said to Eve, "I know
a place where we can hide. There is
a thicket in the northern part of the
garden. It is very dense, and I know we
can hide inside it." He took Eve's hand,
and they ran together for the thicket.
They reached it just as they heard God
descending into the garden. The dark
ones around me shrunk away from the
brilliance that illuminated the garden.
All of them vanished, leaving the dark
one standing close to me holding my
chains. "We will stay." He sang to me,
with a dark grin twisting his face. "I have
won here today. I will stay and show
God what I have done to Him." Adam
and Eve cowered in the deepest part of
the thicket. I could still feel a glimmer of
Adam's thoughts in my mind, "At least
we covered ourselves. I hate this woman
for what she has done, but now was not
the time to worry about that. Maybe
God will leave us alone… maybe He will
forgive me." Adam's thoughts were so

dark, and they were twisted, holding no care or concern for Eve at all, only for his own wellbeing.

Eve began to sob again, and Adam wrapped his arm around her, holding her cold skin against his. It was not a gesture of love but now one of possession; she was his and he would protect her.

God spoke from where He was walking, "Where are you, Adam?" Adam heard his voice with his ears, but I knew that the words did not echo in his heart anymore. Adam knew that he had to face God. "Come." Adam whispered to Eve. "Let's get this over with." They slowly stood to their feet and emerged together from the thicket. As they reached the open area, God stood waiting for them. They held their heads low to the ground in shame. Adam could not feel how much God still loved him. The chains kept him from seeing that. They separated Adam's mind and heart from God. Adam couldn't feel anything from God.

As I knelt there next to the prideful dark one, I felt God's love thrumming out from Him. I felt the pain He felt as He watched His beloved creations approach him. I felt His heart breaking at what He had to do now.

I cried out to Adam, "He still loves you!" I yelled it with all my being. I wanted this to end differently... I wanted Adam to see what I could see. I wanted Adam to feel the love that God felt. But it was useless. Adam couldn't hear me. He couldn't see me. He was completely cut off from this side. I wanted him to see how different things could be if he just asked God to forgive him. I wept loudly into my hands.

I cried out to God, pleading with Him, "It wasn't him! It was me! I ate the fruit! I hurt you! I disobeyed. It was me!"

The dark one threw back his head and laughed at me. He mocked me, "You did it! You gave yourself to me! There is nothing your GOD can do now."

Then I felt His still, small voice echo in my mind, "Do you trust me?" The question came again. Do I trust him? I settled my heart and watched.

Adam answered God, "I heard you walking in the garden, and I hid myself because I was naked. I was afraid of what you would do to me."

"And who told you that you were naked?" God asked. "Have you eaten from the tree I told you not to eat of?"

I felt God's heart break. He knew what they had done. He felt the pain of the separation from his creation.

Adam's mind raced. He knew he couldn't tell God the truth. He knew but he didn't want to admit what he had done. He thought fast. He had to answer Him. He was still holding tight to Eve's arm and then he remembered that she had given him the fruit to eat. That was his out. He shoved her toward God and cried, "She did it! This woman you created for me, she gave me the fruit and told me to eat it." His anger at her spilled from his lips as he accused her, and all the hate he felt toward her returned. He didn't want God to blame him for what he had done. He was determined to make God see that it was His fault, because He had created Eve for him. He would have never eaten the fruit if she had never been created.

Then God asked Eve, "What is this that you have done?"

She cowered before Him and cried, tears pouring from her eyes, "It was the serpent that deceived me.
I ate the fruit because of what he had said to me. He deceived me!" She turned her head away from God in shame.
Then God said to the serpent, which sat close by, "Because you have done this, you are cursed above all other livestock and all other wildlife. You will crawl on your belly and eat the dust of the earth all your days. I will put hatred between you and the woman, between your offspring and hers. He will crush your head and you will strike his heel."
Then God spoke to Eve, "I will make your pains in childbearing very severe; with painful labor you will give birth to children. Your desire will be for your husband, and he will rule over you."
Then God turned to Adam and said, "Because you listened to your wife and ate the fruit from the tree about which I commanded you, 'You must not eat from it,' "Cursed is the ground because of you; through painful toil you will eat food from it all the days of your life. It will produce thorns and thistles for you,

and you will eat the plants of the field. By the sweat of your brow, you will eat your food until you return to the ground, since from it you were taken; for dust you are and to dust you will return." I watched as God pronounced justice with a heavy heart. I felt the pain and hurt from Him... but there was hope still. It was a knowing in God. A light that shown in all this darkness. There was a plan. God knew it.
The dark one tugged at my chains and cried out to God, "I have won! I've deceived your precious creations! I did it! I told you I would." God ignored the dark one's rant.
I watched as God brought animals to where He was and sacrificed them to make clothes to cover Adam and Eve. This was the first time this had been done. I heard God say, "Now they have become like us, knowing good and evil. They must not be allowed to stay here, where they might eat from the Tree of Life and live forever."
I watched, tears streaming from my eyes, as God cast them out of the garden and into the world. They would have to

struggle and strive to survive away from the glory and splendor of the garden. God placed an angel at the entrance to the garden to keep them out and placed a flaming sword that flashed back and forth guarding the way to the Tree of Life.

When all of this had finished, I was left kneeling in chains next to the dark one. He sang his victorious song and continued to mock me for what I had done. He turned to me and bent down to look into my eyes. He grinned and whispered, "You were here. You did this. Because of you, death now reigns and all the beauty that God created for your kind is gone. Now you are bound to me. You are mine."

"Take me back!" I begged him. "I've seen enough! Just take me home."

He threw his head back and laughed, "You chose this! You gave yourself to this! You were there! Don't forget that for now you are mine! You'll do what I want you to do, and oh, there is so much more for you to re-live."

He took hold of my chain and jerked it forward. I was falling again through time and through space. My mind swirled. I was broken. I was owned. It was my doing. I chose this. I waited to see where this journey would bring me next and dreaded where it would take me.

BETRAYER

I watched time pass as I fell. Then I hit
and opened my eyes. I was standing in
an ancient city. I looked down. I wore
a simple robe with a belt tied around
it. The memories of my life faded from
my mind and new memories of a life
overlaid all I had known. I was losing
who I was again. New memories and
a new life enfolded me. The dark one
was close. The chains were still there. I
looked up and remembered why I was
standing outside this great house...
money.
I knocked on the heavy door, looking
around to make sure I wasn't followed.
There was a click and the door swung
open a bit. A servant peered out and
asked, "Who is it? What do you want?"
"Tell the High Priests that it is Iscariot.
I have come to give them what they
want. Tell them I want to discuss Jesus
with them." I answered softly, to not
be overheard. The servant nodded. He

disappeared, closing the door again behind him. I waited there in the alleyway watching the sun fade from the sky above the city. Jerusalem was quiet tonight. So, they want to find a way to get rid of Jesus, I thought.

Maybe I could make a quick coin from this. I had been a follower of Jesus for a few years now and knew that this was my ticket to wealth. I had listened to his ramblings, to all his teachings. What had I ever seen from it all? Where was this kingdom He spoke so often about. Sure... He performed miracles, but was it all worth it, the constant travel... place to place and still no kingdom to call home. No majestic palace to live in. No place to call home. I was tired of all this. I needed money to get what I wanted. I deserved it... after all.

The door in front of me swung wide and the servant motioned for me to enter quickly. He led me through the large house to a room where the high priests sat around a large table. The officers of the temple guard were also there. All of them waited for me. I approached the table and stood at one end and waited.

After a while the high priest spoke first, "We want to get rid of Jesus... quietly... somewhere away from the crowds. We are... tired... of hearing him preach against us, against our city, and against our way of life. He challenges all that we believe. All that we hold dear. He claims to be the Son of God. And that blasphemy... we can NOT allow to continue." I listened quietly as he spoke. When he finished speaking, the others around the table nodded their agreement.

"And what's in it for me?" I asked.

"Name your price." the high priest replied.

A smile twisted my lips as I replied, "Coin and lots of it."

The high priest looked around at the others. Each in turn nodded to him. He looked back at me and answered, "Very well."

He stood from the table and walked over to a golden box that sat near him on a pedestal in the corner. He lifted the heavy lid and reached inside. I heard the familiar sound of coin-against-coin as his hand plunged in. Something like pain shot through me. I recovered. The high priest pulled from the box a handful of bright, shining coins and walked over to where I stood. He stretched out his hand over the table and let the coins drop one by one onto it. He counted as he did this, "One, two, three..." He continued to count, and my eyes widened. This was more coin than I had ever seen before and all I had to do was turn Jesus over to them for it all to by mine. This was much easier than I could have ever thought. I smiled to myself. They really wanted Jesus gone.

When he finished dropping the coins out on the table in front of me, he said, "Find a time and place when Jesus will be alone, away from prying eyes... and then we will take care of the rest."

The high priest returned to the box, dropped the remaining coins back into it from his hand, and returned to his place at the table.

I took my money pouch from inside my robe and placed the thirty silver coins inside it. "I will do what you ask." I replied. I bowed low and turned to leave.

"Oh, and one more thing..." the high priest added,
"Tell no one you were here."
I nodded without turning around and left the building. I hurried back to where Jesus and the other disciples were preparing for the Passover Feast. If anyone had known I was gone, none showed it. I watched and waited for a time where Jesus would be alone and away from the crowds.

The day and hour came for us to sit down for the Passover Feast that Peter and John had prepared. The twelve of us sat down around a long table in front of the feast that had been laid out. I reclined next to Jesus. I kept Him always close. I didn't want to show that anything is wrong. We all talked and laughed together for a while as we ate and celebrated the Passover Feast. Suddenly, as we ate, Jesus spoke up, "Truly I tell you that one of you will betray me." There was such heaviness in his voice. My heart froze in my chest. How could he have known?

The eleven went into an uproar, each saying that it couldn't possibly be them.

I reached out my hand and dipped my hand into the bowl at the same time as Jesus, when He spoke, "The one who has dipped his hand into this bowl with me will betray me." He knew. I was instantly furious, and exclaimed loudly, "Surely you don't mean me, Rabbi?" He looked into my eyes and there was such pain there as he replied, "You have said so." I was silent the rest of the meal and more determined than ever to find a time to turn Him over to the high priest. To say I would betray Him, and in front of all the rest of the disciples. Did he not trust me? Was that how He felt? My mind twisted and churned. I was so angry I couldn't think. I worked hard not to show my feelings on my face. Jesus broke bread drank the wine and talked at length of his broken body and blood. I was in a daze. As soon as the meal was finished, Jesus and the rest were going out to the Mount of Olives. I slipped away, hoping no one would miss me. I knew that later they would be going to Gethsemane, which would be the perfect place to hand Jesus over to them. I rushed through the city and returned to the house where I had met with the high priest before. I knocked quickly and was allowed to enter. The high priest met me at the door.

"Have you earned your coin yet?" He asked me.

"I have. Tonight... Jesus and his disciples will be at Gethsemane. That will be the perfect place to take him without the crowds around." I replied. "And how will the men that we send with you know which man is Jesus?"

I thought for a moment then answered, "I will kiss Jesus and that will be the signal that it is Him." The high priest smiled deeply and said, "Very good. I will form a mob and you will lead them out tonight. Wait for a bit here until I have gathered those I've chosen for this task. Have the servant bring you some wine." He paused and, smiling deeply, added, "You've earned that luxury tonight." I drank the wine that the servant brought me. It was a fine vintage and curbed my anticipation of what was coming. There were suddenly flashes in my mind, flashes of another life far away. I shook my head and it cleared. I waited a long while as the night deepened outside. I heard the high priest approaching and stood to my feet from where I sat. "They are formed up outside. They know what they are to do, and they will follow your lead. Go and lead them to Jesus for us." He said.

I simply nodded my understanding and left the house. Outside there was a very large mob formed. They had swords and torches in their hands. I knew that this large of a crowd would not be needed, but I knew better than to argue that now. I told them to follow me, and we left to go out to Gethsemane. It was dark out and the moon was high and bright this night. There was a dark stillness to the air as we walked through town and out to where Gethsemane was. As we approached, I saw Jesus standing close to his disciples. All the disciples were asleep on the ground.

I heard Jesus exclaim to them, "Are you still sleeping and resting? Look! The hour has come, and the Son of Man is delivered into the hands of sinners. Rise! Let us go! Here comes my betrayer!" As he finished speaking to them, he turned

to face me as I walked straight up to him.
I looked him in the eyes and said,
"Greetings, Rabbi!" and kissed him.
"Do what you came for, my friend" Jesus
replied. A force slammed me in the
chest, and I was tugged backward out of
Iscariot. The chains around me pulled
me back and down again to my knees.
The dark one stood next to me holding
tight to my leash. "Look what you've
done!" The dark one sang into my ears.
"Look at what you are, you and all of
mankind, betrayers!" He mocked me.
There was nothing I could do. I knelt and
once again tears of pain began to sting
my eyes and ran down my cheeks. I had
betrayed Jesus. We had all betrayed him.
I took the coins of silver and handed my
Lord over to them. I was to blame. It was
my sins that turned him over. I started
to weep and struggle against the chains.
I had to do something. I had to save
Him. The dark one laughed aloud at my
struggles and continued to mock me.
I saw now with my eyes opened. Behind
Jesus were angels. They were bright
and shining like the sun. All of them had
their swords at the ready. All were ready

to step forward at the slightest word
from Jesus to save Him, but they didn't
move. All they could do is watch in
horror. Behind where I knelt stood the
dark creatures from the field. Each of
them cried out in victory. They mocked
the angels for not being able to save
their precious God. I watched helplessly
as the crowd stepped forward, took
Jesus by the arms, and arrested him.
As they did this, one of Jesus' disciples
took a sword and struck the servant of
the high priest and cut off his ear. The
man shrieked in terror and fell to the
ground holding the side of his head.
Blood poured out from the wound. He
wailed in agony. "Put your sword back
in its place." Jesus told the disciple, "For
all who draw the sword will die by the
sword. Do you think I cannot call on my
Father, and he will at once put at my
disposal more than twelve legions of
angels? But how then would the
Scriptures be fulfilled that say it must
happen in this way?"
Jesus bent down and touched the
servant's ear, and he was healed
instantly. Jesus then turned to the

crowd that had taken him and said, "Am I leading a rebellion, that you have come out with swords and clubs to capture me? Every day I sat in the temple courts teaching and you did not arrest me. But this has all taken place so that the writings of the prophets might be fulfilled." As soon as He finished speaking, his disciples all fled from there leaving Jesus alone with the mob. They led Jesus off to be taken before the high priest.

I watched them lead Him away. That's all I could do. I was being tossed around like a toy, captive in chains... forced to re-live all these events as if I were the man doing them. My heart was crushed, torn in two by all I had done with my own hands. All my life, I had read about these events with such detachment. Now I was faced with what had been done, not through words on a page, but through this re-living of them. I sank my head to the ground. What have I done? I was separated from God, bound in chains to my captor. I was at the mercy of the dark one. I was sure the worst was yet to come. There was a tug on my chain. I was dragged to my feet. The scene around me dissolved and was replaced with the temple courtyard. It was very late at night. There were many people gathered around the few fires that blazed here. I recognized where this must be. Peter. My mind raced. Not this. Not another betrayal. I turned to the dark one and sank to my knees. "Please no!" I begged him.

He laughed at me and mocked me. He gripped my chain close to where it was attached and, with strength beyond what men possessed, he lifted me from my feet. I dangled there in front of him. Our eyes were level. "You wanted this," he hissed, "You were here! You did it! Now go!" And with his last word he pulled back and flung me toward a group of people huddled around one of the fires. I dissolved into one of the men standing there. His life enfolded mine. Memories of who I was once again faded… and I became the man.

I blinked my eyes. The smoke from the fire was burning them. Tears ran softly down my cheeks. I rubbed them away with my arm. Jesus, the one I loved, and my master was inside facing trial by the chief priests. I was too scared to go in. I didn't want anyone to know I was with Jesus. I was afraid of what they would do if they knew who I was. All I could do was wait. Time passed. People came and went. The fires began to burn low.

A servant girl walked up to me and said, "You were with Jesus of Galilee?" All those gathered around us looked my way as she asked her question. I looked back around at them.

"I don't know what you're talking about." I replied to the girl.

I stood up and walked out to the gateway. There was a crowd here as well and I tried to blend in with them and wait. Another servant girl that had seen me walk up exclaimed to those around her as she pointed at me, "This fellow was with Jesus of Nazareth."

I was angry now. I looked her square in the eyes and swore, "I did not know the man." I put my back to them and looked for another place to wait. A little while later a group of those there walked up to me and said, "Surely you are one of them; your accent gives you away."

I had had enough of this. No one seemed to get it. I wasn't with Jesus. I started to swear and curse. I cried to them, "I don't know the man!" As soon as the last word had left my lips, a rooster crowed in the distance and I remembered what Jesus had said to me, 'Before the rooster crows, you will disown me three times.' My heart tore in two in my chest. I ran from the courtyard and fell to my knees outside.

I wept bitterly. I had betrayed Jesus three times.

Once again, I was torn from the man by my chains, pulled backward and onto my knees. The dark one laughed loudly. "You were there! You were the one!" He mocked. He pulled on my chains, and they dug deep into my skin. The pain I felt didn't compare to what was raging inside me. Once again, I had betrayed Jesus and turned my back on Him. It was my fault. I bowed my head and wept. I couldn't take any more of this.

"Oh... don't cry my pet." The dark one hissed, "The best is yet to come."

The darkness that surrounded me was so thick I could taste the foulness in the air. It burned my lungs. I choked on it, and it seemed to claw its way inside me. I was assaulted on all sides. The mocking creatures were back. They clawed at me and pointed, all rejoicing with their laughter and cries.

My ears stung with the shrieks they made. "Time to see more!" The dark one exclaimed and yanked my chain forward. Again, I was falling into time and space. This fall seemed shorter... much shorter.

WHIP

I opened my eyes and I tried desperately to cling to my memories and my life. I thought about my house, the field, and anything I could remember. I struggled to keep myself intact. I tried to control my thoughts... focus on them, but they were fading again. They were overlaid with another's life. Blended... no... they were overtaking me. I closed my eyes again and opened them.

I reached down and brought another splash of the cold water to my face. It had been a long day. Trial after trial, prisoner after prisoner... my arm was getting sore. I dried my hands and rubbed my bicep. It burned from all the floggings today. "Can't we just kill them without having to torture them first?" I thought to myself. I bent over the crude water pail. It sat in one corner of the common room of my barracks. I looked around at the other soldiers that rested. All of them looked tired from the long

days' work. Why did I sign up for this?
"Hey Marcus!" One of my fellow
Centurions, Kilian, yelled from the
doorway as he entered the room, "Looks
like you got another one! Lucky you!
What does that make for you today?
Five? Six?" He laughed to himself at
the scowl that must have been plainly
visible on my face. He crossed the room
to lean against the wall near me.
"This will be six. I think. I lost count." I
replied, turning to face him. "Who is it
this time? Murderer?
Thief? God forbid, a rapist?"
"A man named Jesus. Doron told me that
he claimed to be the King of the Jews.
Imagine that! He's nothing though, just
another teacher from Galilee... I think.
The high priests hate him. So, he must
have done something horrible or just
made them mad. Doesn't take much you
know!" His smile always seemed to calm
me. He was young and had just arrived
at our company some months ago. I
liked him. He wasn't jaded yet, like I was.
I laughed and quipped back, "King of
the Jews, you say? Haven't whipped one
of those today. I guess... I can take out

all my anger at Caesar on this guy." I
hated Caesar, our current King. Endless
wars and taxation were the reason I
had joined the legion in the first place. I
had to pay my bills somehow and I was
strong and still young enough to know
that hard work paid off in the end.
"Yeah, well... Pilate asked the crowd if he
should release that murderer Barabbas
or Jesus to them. They shouted Jesus.
They chose a murderer over a teacher."
Kilian exclaimed, shaking his head in
disbelief.
"Imagine that." I answered.
It wasn't my job to decide or care about
politics. I just carried out my orders, like
any good soldier would. That was my
job... and I did it well. Across the Roman
Empire, I was known for bringing as
much pain as possible to a man, without
killing him, through the skillful way
I handled my whip. Another soldier
entered the room and yelled to me that
they were bringing Jesus down to the
courtyard for his flogging and I should
hurry and bring my whip. I rolled my
eyes.
"Back to work." I said to Kilian, as I

slapped him hard on the back. "Let's get this over with, then maybe we can get some grub. I'm starving." Kilian smiled back, nodded, and replied, "I am hungry." He then trotted off to ready the ropes that would hold the prisoner in place while I did what I did best.
I walked over to a table where my whip lay and looked down at it. It had been handcrafted and boasted a full seven arm-lengths of hand-woven, braided, and black hair. At the end of the whip, it split into eight different shorter tails. Each of its eight tails had been covered in tiny shards of anything metal and sharp. It wasn't a tool for training horses anymore... now it was an instrument of torture... my instrument. There was still dried blood on the end of it from my last victim. I took it by the handle and let the length of it slide off the table and onto the ground. I flipped my arm up and let the whip slide gracefully into the air and then with a sharp motion I brought my arm downward. The familiar sharp crack filled the air and echoed throughout the small room. It had taken months to learn how to wield this deadly tool and

even longer to perfect that crystal clear sound that sent chills down the spine of even the bravest man. I rolled the whip up and placed it on the hook that stuck out from my thick leather belt. I walked over to my bunk and grabbed my black hood. I wore this to protect my identity as I carried out my task each day. Should any of the family or friends of my victims see who I was they could retaliate against me or my wife and kids. I felt safe behind the mask... and I became different person when I wore it. I was a tool of punishment and I carried out justice on those who had wronged society. I was ready. I heard the crowd outside roar, as now, without a doubt, the prisoner was being readied for his flogging. 'King of the Jews,' I thought. 'First time for everything.' I stretched my arm, feeling the muscles tighten and release. I walked out the door and into the fading sunlit courtyard. All around above me in the stands that surrounded the courtyard were people and it seemed like more than the usual crowd were here to witness this one.
In the center of the courtyard stood a

wooden post that was anchored deep into the ground. With arms raised, the prisoner stood tied to the metal ring that would hold him in place. He wasn't looking at me but leaned against the wood facing away. His back was exposed to me. His bare skin exposed…. my target.

Most all the prisoners that I flogged would have been begging and pleading with me, but… this man was silent… almost peaceful as he waited. Did he know the pain he now faced? Did he feel he deserved it?

I took my place, exactly twelve paces from where he was tied. I looked down at the ground. My boot prints were clear and visible in the dust. A wind blew through the courtyard and a chill passed over me. I looked back up at this man. Something was different, something strange. This was no ordinary man.

I removed the whip from its hook, held tight to the handle, and let it fall to the ground, like a snake uncoiling from my side. I shifted the handle in my hand, feeling the wood and the leather. I got a firm grip on it and shook it out.

All above me the crowd cheered, mocked, and yelled for me to get on with it. They shouted in waves, their energy peaking and their hatred spilling over. They were in a rage. 'Did they even know why they hated this man?' I thought.

I took a step back with my right foot, swinging the whip as I did so. It was a fluid motion; one I had done countless times before. My body moved with the whip and the whip became an extension of myself. I felt the rage and hatred from the crowd fill the whip... and it became the arm of each man and woman there. The whip flung up and behind me into the air, and when it reached its peak, I flung it to its task. It sang through the air and the loud familiar crack rang through the courtyard.

I watched as I had so many times before, in an instant the metal talons of the whip's tail tore through the man's back. He screamed in agony. The sound of his cry rang through the courtyard. The pain in the air was fuel for the crowd's rage and they went wild. They laughed and pointed, some were crying out, "All hail the King of the Jews! Where is his army now? Save yourself Messiah!" I drew the whip back across the sand, leaving a bloody trail as it went. I watched the man. He was still quiet and hadn't said a single word. No begging still. No cries for forgiveness from the crowd. I knew nothing about this man, except that he was brought to me for this, but even still there was something odd about him. The other soldiers that were surrounding the courtyard and watching were mocking and crying out at this Jesus as well. They were going with the crowd. Who was this man?

I stepped back again, bringing the whip to bear again, and let it fly. It sang, cracked, and tore into the man again. Stripes of blood were clearly visible, a blood-soaked crisscross on his back. I continued… thirty-seven more times. Each time he would cry out in pain, the crowd would go wild, and the soldiers mocked him. I wondered if he had family in the crowd above. Was he alone here? Where were his friends?

I turned away from him.

My task was done.

I walked to the edge of the courtyard and set about to washing the blood from the whip. I turned as I washed and heard my commander call for all the soldiers there to circle up around the prisoner. I obeyed, standing to my feet. I rolled up the whip and hung it back on the belt hook. I fastened the clasp so I would not lose it. I joined the other soldiers that were circled up in the center of the courtyard around the prisoner.

They had taken him down from the whipping post, stripped him naked, and placed a scarlet robe on him. He stood; now he wobbled in the center of our circle. The soldiers were laughing and hooting. They bowed low to him crying out, "All hail, the King of the Jews!" They spit on him. I watched as they mocked him and screamed profanities at him. It sickened me.

The energy from the soldiers was contagious. I had pride in my country and hated to think that anyone would try to become King. I felt the hatred of this man pass through me in waves. My mind gave in to the hatred.

"Hail King!" I shouted at him. I was

enraged now and ran forward and spit on him. I bowed to him and, looking up to him, I said, "Hail the King of the Jews!" My fellow soldiers were all following suits. We mocked him and bowed to him. We laughed and joked with each other.

All through this Jesus was silent... almost calm. I could change that! I looked around and called to the other soldiers, "He's missing something? Isn't he? What's he missing? What would a King wear?"

They all looked back and forth to each other, then someone yelled, "A crown! He's not wearing his crown!"

My eyes narrowed and I got close to the prisoners face and whispered, "Exactly, your majesty... let me craft your crown for you."

I turned away from him and walked over to the edge of the courtyard where the vines and thorns wove themselves up the wall. I called for some of my friends to help me. We took the thorn-ridden vines and pulled them loose from the wall. The thorns dug into my skin, drawing blood, and yet I didn't feel the pain. I was enraged now. We wove the thorns into a circle... a crown... fit for this king. When it was done, I raised it high into the air and the other soldiers all let out a cry.

"Crown him! Crown him!"

They chanted those words over and over, as I strode back across to where Jesus stood. I held the crown in front of me. Blood ran down over my hands from the hundreds of tiny pricks in my fingers and palms from crafting it. I stepped in front of him. I bowed low once again and said, "Here is your crown, your majesty. All hail the King of the Jews." I stood and looked around to all my fellow soldiers. "Bow down to him, while I crown him king!" I commanded them. They all bowed on down. They laughed and mocked.

I looked back at the man. His eyes met mine... those eyes... pain... but there was something else there. Love? Forgiveness? How could he love me? I suddenly hated him more. I felt my blood boil. I raised the crown of thorns above his head.

"I crown you... King of the Jews!" I said,

and, with all the strength I could bear,
I shoved the crown down on his head.
The thorns tore through his forehead. I
watched the blood pour down his face
and around his ears. I stepped back and
bowed again. I watched as one of my
friends walked over with a staff in his
hand and pounded the crown down on
his blood-soaked head with it. Then he
handed the staff to him. He laughed at
him and spit on him saying,
"Your scepter, your majesty!"
"Enough!" My commander cried out.
"Get him back in his own clothes and
let's get him to the hill." I was yanked
backward, separated from the life I
had just re-lived. The chains pulled me
backward and down again to my knees.
I was in shock. I watched them take the
crimson robe off Jesus, put back on his
own clothes, and then lead him away
barely alive... carrying his cross.
What had I done? How long would this
re-living last, how many times would I
have to torture my King, my Savior?
I looked around the courtyard with
my eyes opened to what lay there.
The crowd was mingled with the dark

creatures. Darkness everywhere. Evil.
Hatred. Anger. Pride. The dark one still
held my chain, and he was laughing.
"Look what you've done now! You were
there! Your hands held the whip! Your
choices brought Jesus here! You did it!"
He accused and mocked me, singing his
own praises over and over.
After a time, the dark one bent down
and whispered in my ear, "Everyone
always thinks it was me, don't they?
Everyone is so innocent, aren't they? 'I
wasn't there,' people say to themselves.
Does it make you feel good? Does
it? Knowing that you were born two
thousand years after all this? What
you don't see is the blood on your own
hands." He grabbed my hands and
shoved them into my face. "Look!" He
shouted at me. "Look at what your
hands have done!"
I looked down at my hands. Blood. They
were torn from holding the whip so
tight and there was blood... His blood
was on them. The tiny marks from the
crown of thorns still bled on my fingers
and palms. My arm ached from swinging
the whip. I had done it all. I should have

been the one being whipped. Instead, it was Jesus taking my place. Revelation poured into me, and my soul collapsed under it. Jesus had taken the whips for me. He'd worn the crown that I deserved. He went through all of this so I wouldn't have to.

I wept again. Tears poured from me, and they were hot with the pain and the shame I felt. My heart broke in two. My whole life I had heard the stories and I had read them repeatedly. Those words I'd passed over a thousand times before and now... right in front of my own eyes... I'd watched myself commit the crimes that brought Jesus to the cross... for me!

The dark one slapped me across the face with his clawed hand. "Don't lose yourself now! Don't give up and die just yet! I have more to show you! You have more to re-live... and the best... oh... the best is yet to come!" He screamed the words at me. He howled to the sky, "The best is yet to come!"

The dark one jerked my chain and I fell forward off my knees. He started walking, following the soldiers who now led Jesus away. I struggled to my feet against the chains as I was pulled behind him. The soldiers had stripped Jesus of his clothes and cast lots for them. They had placed his cross on his shoulders and made him carry it. He was half dead from all the punishment he'd endured and could barely carry the huge wooden monstrosity of the cross.

Soon we were on the road to Golgotha. They found a man named Simon to carry Jesus' cross for him. The crowd along the way spit on him and cursed him. They called out for him to save himself, save himself like he had saved so many others. They mocked him and laughed at his bloody, broken form. All I could do was be pulled along in my chains behind the dark one and watch helplessly as Jesus stumbled toward the hill... the hill where I knew he would meet his death. We arrived at the foot of Golgotha. I looked up at the hill. It was surely a place of death and darkness surrounded it now. The dark creatures were everywhere. They taunted the crowd, playing with their minds, twisting their rage-filled thoughts into hateful outcries. The energy of the place was that of a pack of wolves set on blood. The soldiers that led Jesus took the cross from Simon and sent him away into the crowd. They hauled the cross up the hill and laid it on the ground. Two other prisoners were already being nailed to their crosses. Their cries wet the air with fear and pain. I didn't focus on them. I watched Jesus now. He was forced down on his back onto the cross and held there. The soldiers that held him waited.

For what? No… not this!

The soldiers held Jesus down and forced him to lie on the cross and wait. The wood against his back tore at the wounds from the whipping and he cried out. Two soldiers held Jesus' arms outstretched and another held his feet. I knew what came next… and I couldn't watch it.

The dark one jerked my chain again and screamed at me, "You can't turn away! This is the best part! Now you get to re-live… my favorite part!" He laughed aloud and pointed.

I saw him now… a soldier carrying a

mallet walking up the hill toward us.
"No!" I cried out. "I won't do it! Not this!
Please not this!" I begged the dark one
and it made him laugh even more. He
pulled my chain and flung me toward
the soldier. My mind faded and darkness
consumed me again. My thoughts
merged with his. My body became his.
Everything I was melted again. "This hill
is always so hard to walk up," I thought
to myself. My feet struggled to find their
grip on the inclined ground. I shifted
the weight of the hammer in my hand. I
hoped this was the last crucifixion today.
I walked up to where the other soldiers
held the prisoner down and exclaimed,
"Looks like they gave this one a nice
beating. Why kill him? Looks like he's
already on his way there." They looked
up at me and laughed.
I walked up to the prisoner's right hand
and reached in my satchel. I pulled out
one of the iron spikes that we used to
nail prisoners to the wood. It was heavy
in my hand and cold. I liked the way the
metal felt in my hand... solid... heavy...
perfect for nailing criminals to the wood.
I knelt beside the prisoner and placed

WHERE ALL JOURNEYS BEGIN

the spike on his wrist. I pushed it down into the skin. It didn't need to break the surface… just hold it in place.

I raised the hammer above my head and brought it down sharply. The spike drove through the wrist easily and tore into the wood of the cross. The prisoner let out a cry of pain, which I ignored. I was so used to all this now. A few more swings of my hammer and the spike sat deeply enough into the wood to hold the man's weight.

I moved to the prisoners' left wrist and drove the spike in there. More cries of pain and blood. I finished my task by driving the last spike through both of his feet.

"That should hold him up." I said to the other soldiers. They laughed and agreed. I was ripped from his mind and body and flung backward with the pull on my chains. I landed hard on the ground and got to my knees.

The dark one sang out, "Save yourself if you can!

Son of God!" He laughed and mocked. I watched helplessly as they raised Jesus' cross up into the air and settled it into place. Jesus hung there, with blood pouring from the many tears in his flesh and from the places the crown of thorns had pierced, waiting to die.

FINALE

I struggled against the chains and stood to my feet, as I watched my King and my Lord up on the cross. Tears stung my eyes. Everything I had ever done in my life... all the times that I had betrayed Him willingly... all the things I had done knowing full well that I was once again choosing the Knowledge of Good and Evil over sweet communion with Him. I had chosen separation from Him instead of the love He offered. I had brought Him here... to this hill... to this cross. It was me.

My life flashed before my eyes in a second. Each time I chose myself over Him, I heard the whip crack and the blood pour down His back. Each time I told a lie, I heard myself say, 'I didn't know Him!" Each time I took His name in vain, I heard the soldiers mock Him and spit on Him. Each time I hated someone in my heart, I heard the pounding of the nails... His skin ripping

and tearing… the wood crack and
split as the nails drove into his hands
and feet. All my life I had done things
thinking I was innocent, but I wasn't.
That's why He came here, through all of
this, for me… for my life so I could live.
I had sold Him over, kissed His cheek,
denied Him three times, whipped Him
to death, mocked Him, spit on Him,
placed the crown of thorns on His head,
cast lots for His clothes, nailed the nails
into his hands and feet, and finally I
had hauled him upward to the sky like
a criminal. All these things I had done.
I had been there. It was my hands that
had His blood dripping from them. All
my sins had brought Him here… here to
die.
I watched through tear-blurred eyes as
the sky overhead darkened. I watched
Him, watched my savior, cry out to
heaven, 'My God! My God! Why have you
forsaken me?'
And I heard His final cry to heaven and
then… He was gone. Dead.
I sank to my knees… it is finished. The
earth beneath me began to shake. I
heard the soldiers, that were standing

around watching, exclaim to one another, 'Surely He was the Son of God!' All this happened around me, but there, wrapped in my chains, I wept aloud. My heart broke. I had done all this! Pain shot through my heart and my soul. It tore with its claws… deep. I had done this! "Can I ever be forgiven for this?" I screamed at the sky. I let my pain ravage me. I wailed aloud. Tears. Hot, hot tears. What had I done! All He had ever given me was love and I had betrayed, tortured, and now finally killed Him! The dark one threw his head back and let out a cry of victory. All the dark ones standing around echoed his call. They danced and sang in celebration. Darkness consumed us all. Jesus, the Son of God, was dead. The dark one sang, "We have defeated Him! He was so weak! So easily slain! Look what you've done mankind! His blood is on your hands now! He is defeated! He is mine now."

The dark one reached out his hand toward Jesus and chains appeared, wrapping Jesus in death. He pulled the chains, and we all sank into what I can

only describe as the grave. There were
hundreds of thousands of souls here
and all were bound in chains like mine.
For as far as I could see there were sin-
chained souls. This place was not inside
time but was outside of it. This was a
place where every soul ever born for
all time waited in darkness. The dark
one sat on his throne holding the large
chains that bound Jesus in the center of
that place. Every chain, all the chains,
all of them led straight up to Jesus from
every soul there. All of mankind's sins
bound Jesus in death. The weight of the
whole world's sins weighed down on
Him.
Then I saw it... my chains were
connected to Him as well. They shot
out from me and were wrapped around
Him. He held the weight of my sins as
well. Jesus' blood dripped from him and
covered the chains that bound him. That
crimson flowed slowly and covered all
the sins of the world for all of time. I
knelt there watching and waiting. For
three days the dark one celebrated
with his companions. They mocked and
laughed at Jesus, their greatest victory.

The Son of God had been defeated. They had won.

Then my eyes widened, as the purest light I had ever seen poured down from above that place. God was suddenly there, filling that place.

I looked toward Jesus, still and lifeless, chained and bound by all sin. His eyes opened and he looked upward. Light filled his eyes and flowed through his body. He breathed deeply. The light spread through his body and clothed Him in its brilliance. Light radiated out from Him and reached every corner of that place. The dark ones shrieked and cowered away from it.

A voice from the light spoke to the dark one, "The price had been paid. The blood of my Son has covered all the sins of mankind... now release the chains of sin and death to Him."

The dark one shrieked in his rage and the chains in his hand shone bright as the sun. He released them and they fell to the ground and shattered. The chains around Jesus melted away and the light spread throughout the place. Chains begin to fall off everyone.

I watched the light race towards me and hit. The warmth and the love that consumed me almost took me from my feet. I felt it all. God's love poured into me. I understood His plan for the redemption of mankind. I felt His complete forgiveness of my sins... of my failures. The chains that had bound me melted and fell off. I stood to my feet. Light consumed me completely. I shone like the sun or rather I reflected the light that poured out from God. I was completely forgiven... completely made whole in Him.

I looked around that place and everyone there was waking up and standing in his or her own God reflected light. All of them wore bright smiles on their faces. There was such joy there now. The dark one and his creatures were nowhere in sight. I was no longer a puppet bound by my own sins. I stood a free man in Jesus, bought and paid for by His sacrifice on the cross. I knew who I was now. I was a child of the King. I was whole because of what He had done on the cross for me. I saw myself as He saw me, perfect in Christ.

There was a flash of light and everything turned white. I opened my eyes and let them focus. I was kneeling again in the field behind my small house. The wind blew steady over my skin. I looked upward. The night sky stretched out above me. The stars shone with a new brilliance. Everything seemed clearer. I shivered. The memories of all I had just experienced were still sharp and vivid in my mind.

"Now you have seen." God's still, small voice spoke clearly to my mind. "Do you trust me?"

Again, He asked me that question, but this time I didn't hesitate with my answer. "Always... and with the rest of my life." I replied.

A Cry To Heaven

My prayer:

Father, I thank you that you alone are God. There is none like you. I thank you that you do always hear me and that my prayers are heard by you. I thank you for the gift of my relationship with you. I praise your holy and awesome name. I pray this now as you have commanded me to pray. I write these words as you've commanded me to write. This prayer... this cry to you. Let it be heard throughout heaven and to the ends of the earth. Father, bless the nations of the earth. Forgive every single person that walks, that carries your breath in their lungs. Father, you are God. The only God. And from you life comes. In you is all things. I thank you that I am found in you. Pour out your Spirit on the whole earth. Shake the foundations and roll up the heavens. Bring peace and your sword. Judge us all with your love. You alone hold the power of life and death in

i

your hands. Your will alone holds everything in being. Without you God we would not be. I would not be.

So Father as I write this prayer to you... as whoever reads these words passes over them... as each one enters their minds and echoes across the ears of their heart. Have your way. Let your will be done in them. Ignite a fire in them that cannot be quenched without you. Let it echo and churn and smolder. Release a famine in their soul that can only be satisfied with more and more of you. Almighty God... do your work in them. Do your timeless work. Do your mysterious work. Drop the breadcrumbs. Lay the foundations and cornerstones. Be the breeze and the fire. Shake everything in their world... so that they will know that you alone are God. I lift up the name of Jesus, He is your son, The Word, the first and the last, the King of Kings and Lord of lords. Let His name be etched in their soul. Unshakable and unsearchable are your ways. Break every chain. Open every locked door. Silence every lie. Release them. Open their ears and their eyes.

I belong to you. I am your servant. You hear and listen to my prayers. You speak to me. So through your Son's sacrifice for me, that brings you and me together, I ask all this written here. As often as it's read, remember my prayer. Let it be a sweet smell to you. A pleasing fragrance. A worthy offering. I bow my knee. I humble my heart. Allow me death everyday, so that your life can be seen. In Jesus name I ask. Amen.

THE BOOK OF BENJAMIN KARETH

"To Know Him, And To Make Him Known."

The ***Book Of Benjamin Kareth*** has one purpose and one purpose only:

"TO KNOW HIM AND MAKE HIM KNOWN."

The Him is ***Jesus Christ***.

This is the heart, the very core of every single one of the one hundred parts of ***The Book Of Benjamin Kareth***.

This is the meaning of the "***Golden Thread***" that runs from the back of the cover of part one all the way across each spine to the front cover of the hundredth part.

The "*White Thread*" that runs from the back of the first of the minor parts and runs to the front cover of the end of that minor part, signifies a section, season, or specific part of the whole.

No single part of *The Book Of Benjamin Kareth* is meant to stand on its own, all the parts fit together to form a whole. All the parts are like puzzle pieces, fitting together to form the ongoing testimony of a life touched by a relationship with and through the power of the Living God.

The Book Of Benjamin Kareth
"To know Him, and make Him known."

Discover the Ongoing Series

Visit
www.tbobkministries.com
or
search Amazon.com for:
"Benjamin Kareth"
to discover all the books of
The Book Of Benjamin Kareth
series.

THE RING OF FIRE

"And I myself will be a wall of fire around it,' declares the LORD, 'and I will be its glory within.'"
- Zechariah 2:5

The following are the prayers of dedication for this book prayed by children of God:

Heavenly Father, You are the One that alone is on the the throne, only You are to be worshiped. Today I pray from within the depths of my heart that this testimony will bring many lost sons and daughters into Your presence to know who You really are and to know their true identity and also to understand how much You love them. Let this testimony bring healing to those broken hearted and mold them into the image of Your precious Son, Jesus Christ who was willing to suffer beyond cruelty and bled and took our penalty on Him. Holy Spirit, let everyone who read this book find You in it and begin to take small steps into their own journey that You have for them. We bless You Lord and give You all the glory, In Jesus Name I pray. Amen.

Jesus, our friend, Savior, brother, King, Lover of our souls and so much more. We dedicate this book in our hands to be an instrument of deep healing and transformation into the lives of every reader. As Benjamin has faithfully told his story of your rescue, affirmation of his identity as your precious son, and restoration to all that you have destined him to be. Jesus, may we each listen to you, hear your voice calling us to walk with you, day by day, into the plans and purposes that you have for each of your children. All for you Glory, that your Kingdom would be seen, felt and understood on earth, just like it is now in heaven, among every people, tribe, language and nation on our planet. AMEN

I thank you Lord for Benjamin's journey with the wonderful creator God who meets us where we are at in

*our lives and promises to rescue us
from the hands of the Devil. He has
provided for each of us everything we
need to accomplish His plan for our
lives as we commit our lives to His
plan and obey His commandments. I
thank the Lord for delivering me when
I was 37 years old and transforming
me from the pit of sin and death.
Benjamin's life is a mirror of my
conversion from a life which was
twisted with sin and all the things
that were destroying my mind, body,
and soul. I pray that you to find that
you receive Him as your Lord and
Savior receiving all that He has had
in store for you also to grow up and
discover the things that He had planed
for his promised life. Thank you for
coming to Benjamin and delivering
him from the grasp of Satan's sins and
deceptions. Little did Benjamin know
that Satan had plans for him which
would destroy his life in rebellion
and sin as he enjoying the sinful
pleasures of own life. I, right now
in Jesus' name, cancel all these sins
of destruction and other destructive
things in your lives. And I pray all*

*that God had planned for you, will
not be present in God's call on your
lives that was for good from your
creation as His sons and daughters.
My prayer is that by Benjamin's
journey is an example that opens each
of your heart, eyes, minds, emotions,
and deeds so that you will be centered
around God's plan and enjoyment
as the man or woman who He had
created you to be. Resulting that you
don't have to go through any more of
the heartaches and pain for following
Satan schemes and has the original
plan for each of our lives, and I cancel
any stronghold, pain, addiction that
Satan has had a grip on your life.
Thank you, Lord that your words are
true and powerful and the power of
the Holy Spirit which is given by Jesus
freely to each of us to live an abundant
life. I pray for each of you will be
obedient to God's Word and receive
His promises that are true. Matthew
7:7,8 "Ask" and it will be given to you;
seek, and you will find, knock, and it
will be opened to you. "For everyone
who asks receives and he who seeks
finds, and to him who knock it will*

be opened." all for of your needs and health. As Benjamin prayed and gave everything in his life to receive what Jesus died for each of us showing us what that the abundant life is real and powerful. I pray that you can quiet yourselves, listen to God's voice, and can look around to see what you are doing, hearing God's commands and be doers of His word. Thank you for Benjamin's openness in describing his journey that you can too follow as you follow the Holy Spirit. God did not promise us the rose garden, but a life more abundantly as you continue your journey while on earth. I pray that each of you will understand and obey His commandments and receive the same fruitful life and journey that Benjamin is enjoying in his journey. In Jesus' name, Amen.

Lord Jesus Christ, we offer this book, flaws and all, to be for the praise of your glory, goodness, and grace. This story is your story seeking and saving the lost, healing and restoring what was broken, and delivering what was bound. Your thoughts and ways are *as high above ours as the heavens are above the earth. Continue your story of amazing Grace in the lives of all who read. Meet each one where they are, but take them where they could never imagine, for nothing is impossible for you! Let your power and love do the exceedingly abundant and above all they could ask or think for from you, through you, and to you are all things! Yours is the Kingdom, the power, the honor, and the glory forever and ever, amen!*

Abba, Father God, thank you for the treasure you have given Your Son and given me and the rest of the family of Christ named Benjamin Kareth. Let Jesus right now "gird His Sword on His thigh...and ride on for the cause of truth, meekness and justice" Psalm 45: 3, 4on behalf of everyone who reads this book. Father, let the treasures found in Jesus be found by these readers as they read Benjamin's testimony. I ask for their lives to be saved from destruction as they would receive Jesus, the Balm of Gilead, who penetrates the deepest of wounds, lacerations and trauma with liquid love. I pray that as saint Patrick led thousands to Christ, Benjamin's testimony would lead not only hundreds of thousands to Christ but 100,000 would become "his sons"and they will "be princes in all the earth." Psalm 45:16for the glory of Your Name. Finally, as St. Patrick prayed, I pray over Benjamin, author of this book, that his prayer would be Benjamin's constant prayer and the prayer on the lips and in the hearts of those who follow the Lamb behind Benjamin.

'Christ with me,
Christ before me,
Christ in me,
Christ beneath me,
Christ above me,
Christ on my right,
Christ on my left,
Christ when I lie down,
Christ when I sit down,
Christ when I arise,
Christ in the heart of every man who thinks of me,
Christ in the mouth of everyone who

speaks of me,
Christ in everyone that sees me,
Christ in every ear that hears me.'
Oh, that the Lamb would receive
the FULL reward of His sufferings
through Benjamin and this written
testimony of this book be taken to
flight through the ones who will run
with it.
In Jesus' mighty Name, Amen.

Father, may you be glorified through
the transformation into Christ-
likeness that this book will bring to
all who read its pages. Allow many
to receive insight into your unfailing
love for them! May they gain the
ability to see in ways that others often
miss. Let Your will be accomplished
in and through the reading of these
pages. May all who discover these
treasures be forever changed by Your
magnificent love!

Father, you alone are worthy of all
praise, from any mouth, tongue, or
heart. All breathe comes from you.
So I stand and ask for you to use
this book for your glory alone. I ask,

in the name of Jesus Christ, Father your will be done on earth as it is in heaven. Take this book as bread and break it, with our thanks, multiply it to feed thousands, and hundreds of thousands. Put your angels around it yesterday, today, and for eternity. Let what is of you endure and what is not fade away. Thank you for this gift. I dedicate this book to you by the power of your Holy Spirit, and by the name of your Son Jesus.

Father, I pray that you will bring breakthrough to sons and daughters through this testimony of your great love, salvation and deliverance. Yours is the power and glory forever! Amen

---

Dear Lord, Bless the telling of Benjamin's testimony. May it have a ripple affect in the community of lost souls. May they see the Truth and respond. Bring spiritual deliverance to their lives. Empower them to follow, to drop all and follow as the disciples of old had done. Holy Spirit, breathe new life to those who've been walking their journey a while and are weary or discouraged. Continue to change hearts as they walk along the road you have for them. We give You all the glory and honor. Amen.

Lord God Almighty in your name we Dedicate this precious book Allow those who read and are in Need of help to be Inspired and blessed by Every word as they understand the Love of their Heavenly Father, through this book may they come to Know and establish a relationship with the One, True Savior Jesus Christ Learning as they meditate on the way to Eternal Life and not only be Blessed but be a Blessing!!!

For every reader of this book, I pray, much like the apostle Paul, Father that each be given a spirit of wisdom and revelation in their reading that they will know the incomparable and great power towards them who believe. May the lives that are changed from its content glorify You Father, that Your love be spread and cover the earth through this one heart on fire!

Father God we dedicate this book to you and your amazing love and that it might have a penetrating effect on many lives and that you will use it in order to convince and convict many people through your Holy Spirit that you are a God of love who desires to have them a part of your family. We pray that the words of this Book will convict many to come home to a God of love who desires them and has been chasing them as the hound of heaven all their lives to come Home.

May the eyes of your heart open to the glory of God. Let him direct, move and inspire you as you read Benjamin's journey. For this I pray in his name amen.

THE CONCLUSION

"To Know Him, And To Make Him Known."

"Now all has been heard;
here is the conclusion of the matter:
Fear God and keep his
commandments,
for this is the duty of all mankind.

For God will bring every deed into
judgment,
including every hidden thing,
whether it is good or evil."
-Ecclesiastes 12:12,13

"This work is done. What I was told to
do, I did."
-Benjamin Kareth